Christmas 1994
To a special nephew,
love,
Aunt Liz & Uncle John

Atheneum
Macmillan Publishing Company
866 Third Avenue, New York, NY 10022
Collier Macmillan Canada, Inc.
First United States Edition 1989
Printed in Italy
10 9 8 7 6 5 4 3 2 1

Library of Congress Cataloging-in-Publication Data
Foreman, Michael.
    The angel and the wild animal.
    Summary: Sometimes the house is inhabited by a
bright and peaceful angel, sometimes by a wild and
rampaging animal, but most of the time by a little boy.
    [1. Behavior—Fiction] I. Title.
PZ7.F7583An 1989   [E]   88–16822
ISBN 0–689–31492–2

The Angel and the Wild Animal

MICHAEL FOREMAN

Atheneum   1989   New York

Sometimes we have
an Angel in our house.
Most times at night,
and mostly asleep.

But sometimes awake,
a golden head in the dark.

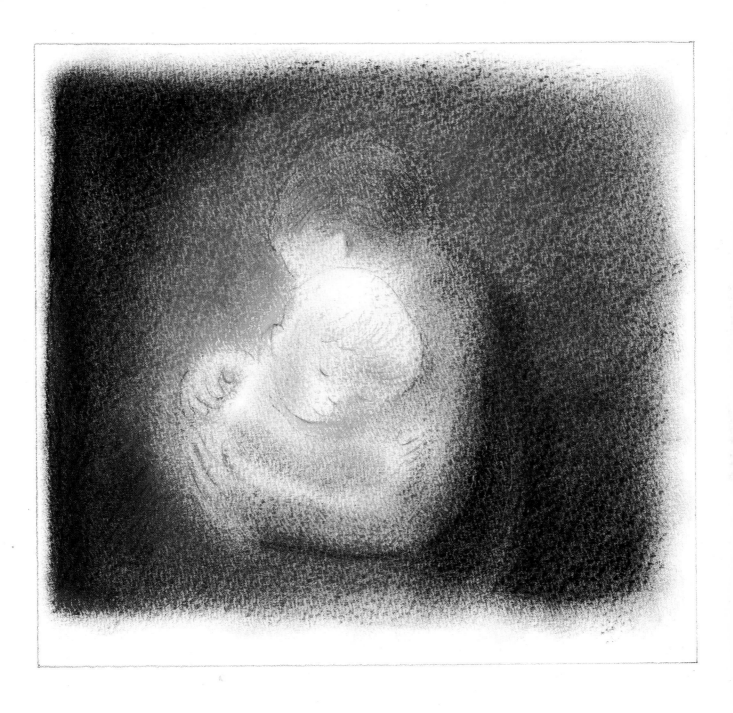

In the day, in the park,
the Angel is brighter
than the sun.

Other times we have
a Wild Animal
in our house.

The Wild Animal
hates the end of a day
and roars against the night.

He wants to live forever

in the rocks by the sea

or in the deep dark wood.

Sometimes the Wild Animal causes floods

and sometimes earthquakes.

Sometimes he makes the whole

neighborhood shake!

And sometimes
the Wild Animal makes
EVERYONE

WILD!

But most of the time we have

a little boy in our house.

These are the times we like best.